<u>SURVIVOR</u>

At the beginning of the ICE-AGE people lived in cave communities where they were able to have some protection from predators. My family lived in a cave smack in the center of ten caves that held close to forty people. There were eight people in our cave when the snow started and the temperature changed, and there should have been at least twelve. Our leader my father whose name was Stone had sent four of our best hunters out into the snow to get meat for our fire. Two of the men Dog and Boy returned with a fat boar, and then they went out on the trail of Horn and Foot the two hunters that had not returned yet. That had been days ago and now food was growing short and Dad was worried; of course, he never told us, I just heard him and mother talking. I was named Scream because mother screamed a lot when I was born; but my sister who was born two years after I was born got the name Simple. Mother always laughed and said after me my sister was a simple birth that's why she got the name Simple.

At this time of my life, I liked to stand at the entrance to our cave and watch the other cave dwellers that lived nearby doing whatever it was they were doing. I also watched with anticipation for the hunters as they returned carrying the different animals they had killed for our fires; and the changes in the weather that up to now had been few, were now big changes. Stone my father finally decided that the four remaining men, he being one, who could hunt should go and find the other hunters that had been sent out first. Dad then kissed mother and me and Simple goodbye and headed to the cave entrance; while one of the hunters kissed his wife and then turned picked up his bow and arrows and met up with dad. The final two hunters had no family and had told Dad they would meet him at the stream near the start of what we all called the Badlands. Then with a wave of his hand Dad was gone off to find and bring back the other hunters. It now became a very serious problem for me; as I now was the only remaining man in the cave. Mother said the rats in the back of the cave have eaten most of our food stored there, and she asked what can we do for something to eat now. I was thinking about a solution to our problem while I looked at the women in the cave; all of them were dressed in animal skins with fur boots and bare arms. I was sure that if we had to eventually leave our home, our clothing would not be warm enough. It was while I was taking all of this in I saw a large rat run over to where Simple was and she hit it with a stick and killed it. I noticed that after killing the rat she threw it over near our garbage pit; as food was short rat became our meat.

It happened that Simple was better at killing and collecting rats than any of the rest of us; so that became her full-time job. Mine became the search for plants and nuts and berries that could be harvested from outside the cave. The three older women I had asked to split up the jobs inside the cave, two of them to do the cooking and one to do the tanning of the rats' skins. Then when the cooking was completed they could sew the skins into clothing for arm covers. I then took my spear and ax and went out to see if any of our neighbors were still around as I hadn't seen any of them for days now. At first I found only dead coals in the firepits and cold air in the caves I visited. I went from one cave entrance to another with the same results; until at the very last cave entrance I heard screams and something running. I immediately dropped into a defensive position my father had taught me bracing my spear against a rock and then I called out to the runner. Right away a girl with long yellow hair who looked to be about my age burst from the cave and right behind her charged a large black bear. She ran past me, and as she did so the bear descended on me; however, I was set and the bear landed on the spear burying the spear deep into its chest piercing its heart. That bear died in agony biting at the spear and then it stopped moving succumbing to death.

The girl had I was to learn returned to stand behind me about six feet away staring wide eyed at the bear and then at me. I entered the cave that she had just ran out of, with her following along behind me; what I saw was not promising as dead bodies lay everywhere. But I was quick to see the quality of clothing these people had been making; so I had her gather up as much clothing as she and I could carry and we went back to my home. As we travelled along to my cave I kept looking back to ensure that I could return when I wanted to. Mother was amazed at the clothing and thrilled with the addition of the girl who said her name was Sun. In the morning I had all the people dress in the new clothes and leather boots with fur inside and jackets with skin stitched inside with hair on the inside. Then when everyone was dressed warmly I led them all to the girl's cave and there we cut up the bear, skinning it first and saving the skin. With five women and me it didn't take us long to divide up the bear and carry it home; where we hung the bigger pieces up on ropes to keep them away from predators.

I suppose you could say I had been lucky to have killed the bear and maybe I was a little too cautious about hanging up the meat but I was young. Mother said I would learn and she also noticed how Sun stayed near me all the time; as if she was feeling safe around me. Simple said that I had finally found a mate, and that I should take her to make it right; but mother said I should take time to appreciate Sun's situation. So, I waited for some sign for Sun to know what or when she would accept me as her man. Three days later Stone returned with one of the other hunters; only they were not happy; in fact, they were practically scared stiff. Time Dad said was not on our side because he and Scalp said that the weather was getting worse; and then they said they had found the other hunters. That they said was the good news, then they said they had bad news the other hunters Dad had sent out had been found near a lake where they had been attacked and killed by a wolf pack. That wolf pack Dad said was now on his and Scalps trail and they were coming here to the cave. Dad said he was afraid that he had brought death on us and holding Mother's hands he cried. I had been watching at the entrance and I saw the wolves following along behind the leader. To say that it wasn't my place to plan how we should defend ourselves was a stretch as Dad and Scalp were here now but I burst out with a statement that froze them all in place.

If you want to live listen closely I said, then I told them how, if we built up the entrance to the cave with stones only one wolf could enter at a time. I told them how they could kill each of the wolves one at a time as they entered following the leader. Dad and Scalp jumped to the task and so did the women and in no time at all, only a small opening remained into the cave. The leader of the wolf pack lunged through the hole and was met with an ax in the brain killing her dead. She was followed by a big brown wolf that I speared and killed just as quickly. All told we killed more than sixteen wolves that day and we had more meat than what we really needed. Then Sun who had watched amazed as we killed the wolves went to work showing the other women how to make warm clothing. This then was how we as an extended family survived the beginning of what people called the ice age. Stone and Scalp acknowledged the fact that while they were away I had taken on a man's duties and succeeded. But they said I should now relax and let them guide the family to safer places to live. Sun was now sleeping closer to me and one night she snuggled up tight to my back and put her arm around me. Mother and Dad found us the next morning curled up together and declared us a matched pair. It was quite some time later that we made love to each other and I found out later it had taken Mother and Simple to teach Sun what she should know about a man. I guess you could say many drawings on the floor had been made and then covered to be drew upon again and again until Sun got the message. I was beginning to look forward to our nights when Dad and Scalp told us to pack up; because we are leaving for a warmer area to live. We took everything we could carry and off we went toward the land where smoke and fire seemed to be ever present. Dad said that where you see smoke there usually is fire which mean't we would at least be warmer than we had been in days. It took us more than four days to travel the distance to the land of fire and smoke. Many times, during that trip Sun made love to me and I was beginning to see a change in her. Sun was eating more and she was a lot more careful about how she walked along, making sure not to place her feet where she might slip and get hurt. I asked mother if Sun was okay and mother just smiled and said, don't worry everything is fine. I would find out later that Sun was with child; our child and I was truly happy.

The weather got extremely cold and snow fell continuously now, never ever taking a brake. Stone and Scalp many times went ahead of our little group, looking for the best paths to follow and places to camp; always taking care to avoid areas of danger. During one of their scouting trips one of the young men went down a path to a small stream where death waited at the stream as the water had been poisoned by the thermal vents that fed it. To drink was to die and that is just what he did; then he buckled up in pain on the ground. He thrashed around for close to an hour and then he ceased to move and he peed himself and died. My father and Scalp returned to find us sitting around the dead body and moaning. They then told us we had to move right away or die, as the water was bad and it was giving off poisonous gas. So, with heavy hearts we moved on, up to this time we didn't bury our dead, we just left them for the scavengers to consume. It would be several years later that I as the leader would change that habit and bury our dead. As for now I followed along helping Sun as we traveled away from the death trap that had killed one of our group. Eight of us remained to enter what dad said was a cave that had fresh water and lots of wood to make fires near it. Then as mother and the others settled in, making the new cave into a home; Sun and I set up an area that we could call our own.

I quickly realized that even with all the comforts of home this place had not one bird, animal or bug anywhere around it; something my father hadn't noticed. I went to collect fire wood not too far from the cave entrance and there near a dead tree I found tracks. Returning to the cave I spoke with Dad and Scalp and told them of the tracks which they quickly went to see. As if a fire had entered the cave Dad and Scalp had us all pack up and make a quick exit from it. After we had gone close to a mile from the cave a large sabretooth tiger leaped on mother, killed her and carried her off. We yelled and screamed and threw stones at it as it took mother away. There was nothing any of us could do, just stand and watch as another member of our group died. Life wasn't fair and we were learning the hard way how not to live without a plan. Thankfully I was a lot more advanced in my thinking than the others and after another night of terror on our part, I became the leader. Stone and Scalp had went out to scout and never came back so I and one other male called Dung arranged the women into a column which made it easier for us to defend them. Dung wasn't that bad a fellow and seemed to truly care about what we did. But even though he cared he lost site of danger and was killed as he walked ahead of us. He had just passed a large rock with some snow on it when a large snake struck him on the neck. We of course killed it and the women skinned it out making it ready to cook. During the march I had the women pick up as many different roots, grasses and berries as possible to augment our food stores. Then as we kept moving with the sun in our faces we noticed it getting warmer. Five of us made that first move to our current location; a valley with water and grass and some animals. I thought we could be safe here but as it turned out, a woman was killed and dragged off by a large bear. I was again reminded of my responsibilities as leader and asked the women to give me a while to think what we should do now. Circumstances forced us to move farther and farther south until we arrived at a forested area which had the ability to provide all the necessities of life.

Sun and I were sleeping out under the stars when screams and snarls were heard coming from an area where one of the women were sleeping. Silence followed the screams and we just went back to sleep thinking everything was okay. In the morning shock and sorrow met us as another member of our group was found dead and partly eaten. I now fully understood that safety was not to be found on the ground so I looked for a tree that could be climbed; as it had in times past been pushed over to become lodged against another tree which stood in a larger group of trees.

During the next several days I watched as Sun and another woman were weaving some reeds they found in a nearby stream into ropes. I used those ropes that they were making as a guideline to help us up into the treetops where with the women's help we laced the ropes together making a platform which we could walk on. I also started using my ax to cut branches and fit them together making a floor and roof and walls to protect us during the rainy season. While wild vicious animals roamed the forest floor we slept safe and secure in the tree tops and our current position also gave us an unrestricted view of the forest floor. If we were careful we could drop down on the unsuspecting animals and have meat to eat. The first day after all the building and constructing of walls and floors and rope guides were completed we could be found high in a tree that overlooked an area of grass and a pool of water. This was the perfect spot to ambush and kill something small that could be hoisted up into the trees. I was careful not to make any noise and as I watched a small deer that went to the water to drink. Taking my time, I raised the spear over my head and stepped off the branch I was on dropping down on the deer piercing it through and killing it. The women lowered ropes to me and after I tied the legs of the deer to the ropes and climbed up to them together we hauled the deer up. When the deer was safely hung up in our tree fort we dressed it out and cut strips of meat off it which we hung on branches to dry. Then we took some of the meat down to the ground to cook; there we ate well for the first time in a long time. That was the start of us living much better than we ever had, until Sun who was now very pregnant pushed me to mate with Pearl. I wasn't even aware of her need of affection but during the night it became apparent that she really needed love. I now was a man with two women and no male help in providing for both.

During the next days I heard many different noises which I tried to identify as animals, birds or unknown; yet every now and then I heard something I couldn't identify. One day as I was sitting listening intently with Pearl and Sun I distinctly heard a women yell. I told the women to stay hidden in the tree fort and I went to see where the sound came from. Travelling lightly, I moved from tree to tree until I found myself looking down on a campsite of several women and five men. I dropped to the ground and stood up and was immediately seen and approached; what a relief to hear language I understood. They asked me many questions and finally I was accepted into their camp. I told them of the dangers they faced on the ground and then I told them of our tree fort. They decided it was safer than where they were, because since they had camped they had lost two of their men. I lead them to our tree fort and after all were safely well above the ground I pulled up the rope ladder. They were surprised to find the two women and the deer meat where it hung drying. Together we ate and then built a larger platform for all of us to sleep on. In the morning we proceeded to hunt and collect as many nuts, grasses and seeds as we could carry as twelve of us were now needing food. I became the leader of the group as they were not as smart as Sun and I and Pearl seemed to be. Sun went into labor one night and had a boy much to my relief. Now our group was thirteen strong and I knew from the way our tree fort was cramped it was again time to move on.

After talking to the others in our group and deciding what was best for all of us; we started off early one morning through the mist and fog toward the unknown. I knew if we were to survive we had to stick together. Its funny but none of the men or women had names, so I named them, Stone, Dog, Scalp, Boy and Bone then I went to the women. To my surprize they had decided to name themselves, they became Flower, Twig, Leaf and Sprout. My Son was brought out by Sun and I had asked her to give him a name, she chose Moon to be his name as he was born at night. Our men were placed as I felt in spots where they could defend the women. Yet to my surprize the women teamed up with the men ensuring our safety as we moved on. We had just moved into a heavily wooded area when a large deer was seen drinking at a water seep. Approaching very carefully I used my bow and was pleased to see my arrow pierce the deer right through the heart. The deer jumped and raced across a small opening in the trees and disappeared but only a short walk into the trees found the deer laying down against a stump. It didn't take us long to draw the deer into the open where the women went to work dressing and cutting it up. Others were quickly getting a fire going and cooking the meat; all the while the men stood guard.

For a period of more than six months I led the group through canyons and forested areas always going south. Then we encountered the wet lands; which proved to be a challenge that claimed four of our group. We had been spread out in a long line thank God when four of our people plunged into a deep hole full of quicksand and disappeared. The loss of so many members of our family was a giant blow to us as a group as well as to our feeling of security. I was faced with having to adjust our order of march that very instant and with three members of the group placed together as a working unit we went ahead. Our men and women were made up of three sets of walkers that formed three separate groups; which should something bad happen to one group the others could help them. My big concern was that my group was composed of myself, Sun and our baby which left us vulnerable; should we be attacked by wild animals. As we moved through the water I had a great idea; I put the women to work weaving new rope from the water reeds. Boy oh boy were those new ropes strong and at that point I had members of each group of walkers tie themselves together leaving about five feet between each other. I then thought back to the four members of our group that we lost and I had each group tie a rope from one of them to a member of the other walking group; that way they could pull them out of trouble should it happen again. This system worked well until we left the wet lands and entered the bush areas and then the ropes helped us stay off the ground at night. We set up camp in some old oak trees by tying a rope to a chunk of wood and throwing it into the tree limbs until eventually it stuck and up one of us went. Securing the rope to a good strong limb we all climbed into the safety of its branches or maybe not. As the family settled in for the night out of the branches slithered a large snake which sank its fangs into a young man and then wrapped around him. His yells of pain brought us to his side where we killed that snake; however, the poison that had entered his body killed the young man. I know this will sound callous but we didn't know any better at that time; his friends just picked him up and threw him off the branch he was on, to fall more than thirty feet to the ground.

As I stood there watching this take place I felt a sense of despair as his broken body lay crumpled on the ground far below. The next day brought its own problems as our family found out that our friends' body was gone and in its place stood a large bear. Never had I ever seen men and women attack and kill a bear that would normally kill most of them without effort; yet now they all worked together as a solid fighting unit and the bear had no chance. Days later with plenty of bear meat to eat the eight of us decided to move farther south to a warmer area. I knew we weren't the only family to go south to warmer areas to live; which proved to be a totally different problem for me to have to overcome. During this time the women who had no mates began looking more and more at the men in our group; until finally they just took up with every man they could.

During that time in our lives we found many animals that we normally hunted at home had moved south ahead of us; as if they knew more about what was coming than we had. This knowledge helped us to realize that our lives depended on the animals and where they went we should go also. Then came the day of heart brake and confusion for me; because I was not what one would say a violent man. As I remember it we had been hunting when Sun brought my attention to men who were cutting up a deer near some water. At first all I saw was people who had been successful in a hunt and then I saw one of them throw up his arms and fall forward on his face. Then a lot of yelling took place and more of that group of hunters fell onto the ground. I couldn't see just what had taken place until I crawled closer and I almost threw up. There walking up to the hunters on the ground were a group of rough looking people dressed in animal skins and carrying bows. They were unwashed and I could smell them from where I lay concealed in the brush; murders of the hunters that had been cleaning the deer.

My first thoughts were to run away then I became fascinated as I watched them strip and start cutting up the hunters. So now I knew these were cannibals, hunters of people for food. Many times, in the distant past Stone my father had told of these people. He told how many groups had gotten together and hunted them down and killed them; all of them that is that they could find. It now became apparent that not all of them had been found and killed by the hunting groups back at that time. I gathered my family together and we discussed what we should do; as we knew that no one was safe if they lived. It was decided that a trap would be set up to capture one of them and then question him about the rest. Sun was to put herself in harms way as the bait; but I had her put some rope lashed together into a blanket that could be worn as an under garment. No arrow fired from a distance could penetrate it and it would look like she had been killed; but in fact, she would be very much alive. The plan was to have one of the cannibals shoot her and then as he went to cut her up we would jump him and tie him up. The plan worked well except that not one but two of the cannibals went after the bait; that left us to tie up two of them. We sat around a fire asking them questions which they said they didn't understand; until I introduced one of them to coals from the fire. It took several hot coals to loosen their tongues but eventually we discovered that they were from a group of ten. They said five men and five women hunted other people in this area killing and eating them, then they took everything they had.

The two men we had captured left their group of eight members no stronger than our group of eight. So, with no more feeling about killing a deer Bone cut their throats so there would be no escape. We all presented our plans on how to kill this group of cannibals and from them we picked the best idea. As these people hunted on the ground we decided to climb into the trees where we could shoot arrows down on them. This would give us a tremendous advantage and then with many of them down or wounded we could drop on them with spears and axes. The problem was how to attack them and then dispatch them quickly while they were confused. I had Bone and Pearl pretend to be in a fight shouting and swearing at each other; then go into the trees after they had been seen. This worked to perfection and later after the killing had ceased we gathered the bodies and for fear of attracting animals we buried them. This then proved to be the very first time we buried the dead. It was I must say a most successful way to prevent animals from coming around eating the dead. We all noticed the results of burying the dead, no bad smells, no scavengers came around and that made us all happy.

We went to the campsite of the cannibals and there we found many weapons and good clothes all made from leather.

As we sorted through the items I discovered some necklaces of shells and gold rings which I gave to Sun. We also found lots of well-made bows and arrows fledged with turkey feathers and pointed with very sharp metal points these we along with axes made of a shiny metal that was sharp. We could hardly believe our good fortune and that night as we relaxed in our tree fort we dreamed of a time when we wouldn't be afraid. The night passed without any disturbances and after the sun rose we ate and left our tree fort to travel ever further south. The sun was hotter or so it seemed and as we moved along it became apparent to me that many of our family needed rest.

Rest for us all came when we arrived at a river that was deep and wide; something we felt could protect our north side of the camp. We set up house keeping around a fire pit that the women built and several of us went out to hunt. Two men and two women stood guard over the camp, ensuring safety for us all. Sun was feeding Moon who had started eating solid food by now and for that we were all thankful. Then as I watched Sun feeding Moon out of the bush came the two hunters carrying a wild pig on a pole and everyone was excited to see them. We celebrated and ate our fill of the wild pig meat and then we all just seemed to slump down into a deep sleep out of exhaustion. It was late the next morning when we all started to move around the fire pit, this was something we had not experienced since we started our trip south. Usually we were up and moving well before the sun rose and were working on weapons and preparing clothing before most of the children were awake. Moon had gotten up and went to the shore of the river to find snails and clams if any were there; however, he didn't notice a large bear that was fishing nearby. Moon was distracted by a large fish that was swimming around in a small pool and with a sharp stick he stabbed it. His shouts of joy at killing the fish were quickly overshadowed by the snarling and bellowing of the bear as it ran towards him. Frozen in terror Moon stood and stared at his approaching doom, one thousand pounds of pure muscle plowed into him. He was thrown about six feet and fell on his back where the bear ripped a large chunk out of his stomach. Sun and I along with the rest of the family descended on the bear hacking and stabbing it to death; but not in time to save Moon.

Sadness once again overshadowed the family group as we buried Moon and then with heads hanging low walked on. Ours was a journey of hope in the beginning but it had declined with one heartbreak after another. I tried to comfort Sun but she would have none of it; preferring to sit alone and eat very little. The other women tried in vain to get her to cheer up and eat but they were not able to get through to her. For the next several days Sun remained in a state of sadness and depression; then as if a light had came on she was again her old self. I was overjoyed when Sun quickly returned to my blankets; which I should have realized was her attempt to have another child. I moved the family farther south until wear and tear had taken all their get up and go away and so they settled in a beautiful canyon with a stream and lots of large trees. Large beautiful trees grew right up to the edge of the stream and overhung the water. The family used their knowledge of ropes to climb up high into the tree tops where with the new ropes and axes from the cannibal camp they built a new home. Sun and I built a new home in a tree close to the stream where they were able to fish right from a platform over the water.

In time other family groups moved into the area and set up camps on the open ground. During one of my hunting trips I came upon a campsite that have been trampled and torn up. As I was looking around I found where the people had been digging in the ground and I also found a skin with what looked like seeds of some kind. In my ignorance I had pulled a handful of the seeds out of the skin sack and having smelled them and tasted them I threw them away. I then proceeded to search for any signs of the people who had lived in the camp. I was totally absorbed in tracking the people who had run from the camp and when I topped a small hill and my heart stood still. Spread out before me was a scene of utter destruction and death. People were laying in heaps, some together but most were thrown around as if by a giant hand. I found men with crushed chests and women with punch marks on their bodies then others I couldn't tell what had killed them yet all were dead; until I heard crying and I found a small boy of about Moon's age.

I searched but found only the dead so I returned home with the boy who didn't talk. After they arrived at the trees I took the child up into the trees and to a new home. Sun was overwhelmed with many emotions as she saw the child and then she grabbed him and hugged him and wept. The boy responded after several minutes and he told a story so amazing that all who heard it could hardly believe. He told how his family had settled in to live where I found them and for many days all went well. Then in a matter of minutes all was destroyed; animals with large horns and shaggy hair had run through their camp. The people were just over a small hill beginning to dig up the sod to make houses when the animals charged through them. All were killed in the stampede and only he remained to tell the sad story. I said that with any luck the family could hunt and kill some of the shaggy animals for food and clothing in the winter. So, it went season after season until the spring when the weather again began to change. The trees were keeping their leaves longer and the sun was stronger making it unnecessary to wear so many animals' skins for warmth.

Our family group had grown to include more than forty other people, some from broken groups and some sole survivors of other groups. Sun and I had never had another child even though we tried and then one day Sun just up and left me; never even saying goodbye. I went through a very bad time after the brake up, but like everything else in my life I managed to survive it. Dad always told us that when times were hard it was no time to give up; so I pressed on with life hoping for better days.

During the years of warming temperatures, I had become a lot more listless and I wanted to return to my old home up north. So, with my weapons at the ready I headed north leaving the safety and security of the family I had started. As I remembered the valleys and streams I had passed on my way south I looked for any sign of others moving north, but as always never found any. It was during a quiet rest I was having by a stream under the shade of a giant tree. Mine was a journey of remembering and as such took me to where my son Moon had been buried. It wasn't too hard to find the exact spot and as I stood looking down at the bare ground I felt something should identify this place. Looking around I could see several big logs but when I tried to lift them I just couldn't do it. Then in desperation I took a stone that was about two feet long form and then I drove it into the ground at the head of Moon's grave. This would prove to be the first time someone had marked a grave with a stone marker.

Having faced many dangers and rough terrain to get to my destination, I had become hard and physically stronger than most men my age. Days later found me approaching the very first tree fort that I had made and I quickly climbed into the tree tops where I found everything just like I left it. I settled in for the night confident of my safety for before I shut my eyes I placed a spear across my chest for quick action should it be necessary. During the night I sensed a presence near me and I although awake was ready to fight. What happened next is still a mystery to me for I felt a heavy weight against my side and then all became quiet. It wasn't until the morning that I realized I had shared a bed with a sabretooth tiger that had a bad wound in its right side. Never one to look providence in the face and ignore it, I went right away to the stream got some firewood blazing and boiled water. It was difficult to get the hot water up into the tree fort but I did get enough up there to wash the wound in the big cat's side. The cat was not pleased with me at first and clawed me down my right arm, thankfully it wasn't that deep a wound. I worked on the big cat three or more times a day and then I fed him meat from a deer I had killed that was drinking at the stream.

When a week had passed I noticed that the cat had moved around a bit; however, I don't think he liked the name Sam that I gave him. At the end of the second week Sam as I called him was gone in the morning when I awoke; leaving me alone once again and on my own. I climbed down to the ground boiled some water and cut up some meat from what was left of the deer. Then as the day was fresh and the air clean I turned north once more; always in the back of my mind the life I had as youngster in our cave. That cave as I remembered it was deep in the mountains where even in the summer the water was cold flowing from the snow on the peeks high above. It was my dream to raise a family and to be able to teach my children about the glorious things I had learned during my travels. Two days of travel and I could see the rock face with its many scarred openings where I had played as a child; then as the day was almost gone I made camp. During the night I was awakened by rumbling and shaking in the earth; then a series of screams and more shaking. I could hardly stand up so I grabbed hold of a tree that was close by and held on tight. The earthquake split the ground before the cave mouths and then disappeared into the rock face. As the trembling of the earth ceased I was going to step away from the tree when another jolt started much stronger that the first one. I was thrown to the ground and bounced around until I was physically sick; then peace and serenity returned. Several large rocks were still falling from the mountain side to go crashing off into the meadow far below. I found myself in awe as I stood and looked at what used to be my home. A large crevasse was where my family cave had been and the caves on either side had been destroyed; all that remained was piles of rock. I went to where the earth had split open and a deep crevasse ran from as far as I could see to the west right up to where my home had been. It was abundantly clear that safety for me was not as I had supposed to be in a cave; but as I had already learned was in the trees.

On the move once again, I travelled east this time and I encountered what I still call heaven; a valley of green grass banked by a large stand of trees and plenty of water. A large waterfall came crashing down from high above in the mountains to form a large pool at the bottom; then the water flowed across the valley floor to disappear into the forest below. I walked into the stand of trees and found where deer tracks went to the water; also, some large predators were in the area as their tracks affirmed. So, working on my own and remembering how the women had made their ropes I fashioned large ropes for connecting the trees and forming platforms for sleeping. Then smaller ropes for tying braces for the roof, walls and then I went to find a suitable tree to climb. As I walked among the trees I was sure something was watching me; but I never got a glimpse of what it was. Then I found what I sought the perfect tree, it grew straight up into the air in an open area and then spread its limbs out in all directions. Its limbs were entangled with other trees near it making a blanket like area in the air. The problem was how to get up that high, so I took a heavy stick and tied it to a rope and after many tries I finally got that stick over a limb. The next problem was that the ropes couldn't support my weight so what could I do. I was stumped so I sat down to eat something and think out what I should do next; however, as I sat there I saw the heavy stick slide down the other side of the limb and come crashing to the ground. I rushed over to the stick and I realized my problem had been solved, I now had a rope over the limb far above. Then I tied a large rope to the end of the small rope and pulled the large rope up and over the limb; as the large rope came back down to me I tied it to another tree and up I went into the tree. As I reached the limb and looked for the first time at my future home I felt secure for the first time in a long time. For the first night I tied myself to a tree limb and slept off and on waking every time I heard a new noise. In the morning I proceeded to cut limbs and tie them into a platform on which I could safely walk. I made walls and a roof then a walkway from my tree to another tree where I made a larger more solid platform and tree fort. The first area was to hang meat that I would get by hunting and for storing nuts, berries, grasses and other items that I found.

It was now time to hunt as all my food stuffs were nearly exhausted. I went to the large pond where the waterfall was creating a mist that soaked everything on the far side. Here on my side I found deer tracks and bear sign created from the animals coming to drink. I took up a position close to some shrubs and waited, eventually a small deer showed up and I was able to bring it down with one arrow. I dressed it out and carried it to the tree where after tying the deer to a good rope I climbed up into the tree. I can tell everyone it was a challenge to get that deer up to the limb by myself and that got me thinking of how I could make it easier to do this. If I was fortunate enough to harvest a larger animal I would not be able to hoist it up into the tree fort unless I used some other means to do so. Thinking ahead I cut a limb of about five feet long that had a tee crotch in it; then I went down to the ground to eat and think of what to do next. While I was eating I saw a log that I had been using fall into the fire and it had a hole in it. I grabbed it out of the firepit and brushing off the burned part I had a four-foot piece of a log with a hole in the centre of it. I was pleased because I could put the pole I had cut into that hole after I tied the log to the tree limb for above. I took the log up the tree and tied it in place; then I placed the pole into the hole in the log. I then tied a stick to the crotch end of the pole and secured it in place. What I made was the first pulley that ever was, and with it I was able to hoist large animals high into the tree tops.

For some time now I had been lonely but recently I realized I was not alone; because something was around watching me. I felt that if it was a human it might be hungry so I started leaving meat at the campfire. For two nights nothing happened and then the meat was gone; what relief to finally realize someone was around. I put out more meat and decided to sit and watch. At about sun down I saw a young woman creep into my campsite and sit and eat the meat; then get up and run into the brush. I decided it was time to find and talk to the woman so I tracked her to a shelter that was poorly built back in the brush. The woman I found huddled inside and seemed to be terrified of something I couldn't see at first because it was dark. Then out of the back of the shelter came a sabretooth tiger; which I watched carefully as it approached me. I noticed an old scar that it had on its side and I hoped that my next decision didn't cost me my life; however, I took meat from my pouch and threw it to the cat. The cat stopped picked up the meat ate it and then came right up to me and smelled me. I said Sam is that you, and as I stretched out my hand to the cat he licked my fingers. The woman at that point seemed to come out of her trance and ran to me throwing her arms around me; while I scratched Sam behind his ears something he had always liked. Seemingly satisfied he moved off out the door and into the bush, me I just stood still as the woman hung onto me in a state of fear.

It took quite a while for her to calm down as she realized she was going to be okay and that Sam was not a threat. Then together we returned to my campsite where she sat and ate some more meat that I had from a deer I had killed earlier. As we sat at the firepit the woman told me her name was Fair and I said my name was Scream which made her laugh. Then I asked her if she had family close by that I could take her to; she replied that she had no-one. Then she said that she had been watching me for a while and wanted to know if she could stay with me, I said yes she could. After that we took off to the forest where I showed her how to climb up into the tree fort and where I hung up the animals I harvested and of course where I slept. She was excited at seeing the tree fort and that night she slept with me safe and secure for the first time in months. From then till now almost ten years have passed and Fair and I have four children and we live safe and secure high in the trees. Of course, we had to expand the tree fort to accommodate our growing family but lots of trees were close enough to do that. I must be clear we have been very successful since taking up residence in our tree fort raising a family and hunting in the valley I called heaven.

I want you to know that I put my life story down on paper so that everyone would understand me. I was a survivor of the cave, the reason burials were used, the tree fort builder, and the first man to mark a grave with a cross. Yes, you could say Scar raised the only survivor of his family well way back then; when he had started the family in the cave in the mountains.